Acting Edition

Heritage of Wimpole Street

by Robert Knipe

I0586964

‖ SAMUEL FRENCH ‖

Please refer to page 39 for further copyright information.

PREFACE

While the persons of this play are authentic, the plot is purely fictitious. Great liberties have been taken with the ages of the characters and the dates of their lives in relation to the period the play depicts.

To be accurate, Edward Moulton-Barrett never saw his grandson, who was not eleven, but nearer sixteen, when he visited England.

Similarly, liberties have been taken with the Barrett sisters and brothers, and the Barrett ancestors mentioned in the play are entirely fictitious.

However, the spirit of the family has been maintained, and the actual character of the elder Moulton-Barrett has been approached.

An interesting feature of the play is that it portrays what might have happened had Edward Moulton-Barrett lived to see his grandson.

Heritage of Wimpole Street

CHARACTERS

ONE MAN   ONE BOY   THREE WOMEN

EDWARD MOULTON-BARRETT, *master of Wimpole Street.*
HENRIETTA MOULTON-BARRETT, *his daughter.*
ARABEL MOULTON-BARRETT, *another daughter.*
ROBERT BARRETT BROWNING, *a grandson.*
JANE, *the maid servant.*

SCENE: The drawing room at 50 Wimpole Street, London, England.
TIME: About 1856. Five o'clock of a winter evening.

Heritage of Wimpole Street

SCENE.—*The drawing room at 50 Wimpole Street, London, England. It is a lofty, high-ceilinged room, darkly panelled in oak, in excellent taste. Candles, in silver candelabra, gleam on the desk and are reflected in the polished surface of the piano.* Flowers relieve the gloom of a room inclined to be somber. The furniture, of Mid-Victorian period, is heavy and uncomfortable, despite its apparent costliness. There are long windows, heavily draped in velvet, at* R. *Through them can be seen the dusk and fog of early evening. A dark, heavy, gold-framed family portrait, in oils, hangs on the wall in the center above the panelling.*

(*At rise:* HENRIETTA MOULTON-BARRETT *is discovered* L. *in the chair beside the desk sewing on a bit of embroidery. Her sister,* ARABEL, *seated* R. *on the sofa, is reading aloud from a small, calf-bound volume of Elizabeth Barrett Browning's poetry.*)

ARABEL.

". . . But the young, young children, O my brothers,
 They are weeping bitterly!
They are weeping in the playtime of the others,
 In the country of the free."

(*She lowers her book and looks out into space.*)

HENRIETTA.

(*She stops sewing and, with needle poised, speaks as she leans forward.*) It's beautiful, isn't it, 'Bel?

* The piano is not essential, and may be eliminated if desired.

11

ARABEL.

(*Intensely.*)   One of the most beautiful things she ever wrote.

HENRIETTA.

(*With pride.*)   We'll never forget Ba, Arabel.   The world will never forget her.

ARABEL.

(*Going in back of sofa and placing the book on the little table.*)   I'm afraid Papa has forgotten.

HENRIETTA.

(*Rising and speaking spiritedly.*)   Don't you think it! He'll never forget Ba.   She was the only one of us he ever cared for.

ARABEL.

(*Glancing about.   Warningly.*)   Henrietta!   Be careful!

HENRIETTA.

(*Walking* c.)   Well, it's true!   He hates us—he always has!   After Elizabeth went away with Robert Browning, he refused to hear her name mentioned again—and why? Not because he loved her less for marrying against his wishes—no, not that!   Just because of his pride—his foolish, arrogant pride!

ARABEL.

(*Softly.*)   He never saw her after she went away . . . and now he never will see her. . . .

HENRIETTA.

Yes, I know. . . . (*Suddenly turning to* ARABEL.) You said he acted queerly when news of her death came ——

ARABEL.

(*She shudders.*)   It was awful!   He opened the letter and read it.   He didn't move an inch—just stood stock still—like a piece of stone. . . . Then he looked up—and crumpled the letter in his hand and dropped it on the floor

. . . he never said a word. It wasn't natural—it wasn't human!

HENRIETTA.

(*Walking* L.) I can just picture it all in my mind. That's exactly what he would do.

ARABEL.

I had hoped he would be more kind—more human after Ba's death.

HENRIETTA.

(*Sitting in chair beside desk,* L.) He's worse, if anything. I sometimes think he *is* made of stone.

ARABEL.

I—I suppose he can't help it. He does what he thinks is right. But he must have felt grief—he *must* have— even though he wouldn't show it.

HENRIETTA.

(*Quietly.*) Perhaps he did. I don't know.

ARABEL.

I don't understand why he hates us so. After all, he's our father.

HENRIETTA.

(*Standing and taking picture from the desk.*) You'd never know we were anything to him but slaves. Ba was the favored one—and he never showed affection toward *her*. But at least he has her picture. . . .

ARABEL.

(*Sitting on sofa. Sadly.*) I don't think he ever looks at it.

HENRIETTA.

If Ba could have known that it has always been there since she went away, I know she would have been happier. . . .

ARABEL.

I know. She tried to see Papa so many times when she

and Robert were in England, and yet he wouldn't even *write* to her.

HENRIETTA.

(*Walking impatiently* c. *and turning.*) Oh, we get so stirred up about Papa! I'm afraid we'll never understand him, or he us. We may as well resign ourselves.

(JANE *enters by door* L. C., *carrying several letters on a small silver tray.*)

JANE.

The post just came, Miss.

HENRIETTA.

Anything for me?

JANE.

Yes, Miss. And for Miss Arabel. (*She crosses* R. *and* ARABEL *takes three letters from the tray.*) This one is for you, Miss Henrietta. (*She crosses* L. *and passes one letter to* HENRIETTA, *after giving it a last lingering look. There are still several letters on the tray. She strains to see over* HENRIETTA'S *shoulder.*) I think—I *think*, Miss, it's from Mrs. Jameson.

HENRIETTA.

(*Opening letter.*) I think you're right, Jane. It does look like her handwriting.

JANE.

(*Crossing* R. *again to* ARABEL.) I *thought* so, Miss.

HENRIETTA.

(*Bitingly.*) You have an uncommon knack of telling people's handwriting.

JANE.

(*Giving up her attempt to read* ARABEL'S *letters.*) Thank you, Miss, I ——

HENRIETTA.

(*Cutting her short.*) Leave any mail for Papa on his desk.

JANE.

Yes, Miss. (*She goes* L. *and puts the remaining letters on the desk.*)   Will there be anything else, Miss Henrietta?

HENRIETTA.

(*Looking up.*)   What?   Oh, no, thank you, Jane.

JANE.

Very well, Miss.   ' [*She exits.*

ARABEL.

(*Putting her letters aside.*)   Nothing of interest.   Bills mostly.   Won't Papa be furious when he sees the one for the new dress?   But I couldn't help buying it even though he *is* bound to be displeased.   Do you think . . . do you think he'll be *very* unpleasant, Henrietta?

HENRIETTA.

(*Troubled.*)   I'm afraid there's going to be a lot of unpleasantness for all of us soon.

ARABEL.

(*Rising and going* C.)   Whatever's the matter?   Tell me, Henrietta.

HENRIETTA.

(*Speaking dully.*)   This letter is from Mrs. Jameson. I've feared something like this.   I've feared it ever since Elizabeth died.

ARABEL.

(*Anxiously.*)   What is it?   What's the matter?

HENRIETTA.

The Jamesons have arrived in England, and they've brought our nephew, little Robert Browning, with them.

ARABEL.

Oh, how lovely!   I'm so anxious to see him.   He must be quite grown up by now.   Almost eleven, isn't he?   I wonder if he still looks like Elizabeth?

HENRIETTA.

(*Impatiently.*) You don't seem to understand. They intend to bring him here—here to this house.

ARABEL.

But ——— (*Suddenly seeing her point.*) Oh, you mean . . . you mean . . . (*After a pause she sits weakly on sofa* R.) Papa?

HENRIETTA.

(*Pacing.*) Yes, yes. Don't you see? Father will refuse to see the child. He'll make a scene—a calm, cold, icy one that the child will never forget.

ARABEL.

But how do you know he will?

HENRIETTA.

(*Sitting* L. *in chair beside desk.*) I know! I *know!* It isn't in him to do anything different.

ARABEL.

But why are the Jamesons bringing Robert? Surely they know about Papa. Why are they in England anyway?

HENRIETTA.

(*Looking down at the letter in her hand.*) They say his father isn't satisfied with the Italian tutor they've had, so he's sending little Robert to England to go to school at Henley. As far as I can make out, the idea of bringing Robert to see his grandfather is entirely the Jamesons'. They seem to have some idea that they can soften Papa— make him forgive Elizabeth through a fondness for her boy.

ARABEL.

If only they could! I'd like to feel that Papa *had* forgiven Elizabeth. And how nice it would be to have a child running in and out of this gloomy old place.

HENRIETTA.

(*Rising and walking* L. *in front of desk, impatiently*

tearing letter.)   Why did the Jamesons have to think of anything like this?   It will do more harm than good—I know it will!   (*Looks at watch.*)   And I can't get in touch with them to stop them—it's too late. Mrs. Jameson says that they'll be here by five-thirty today.   It's already nearly five.

ARABEL.

I wonder if they intend to get in touch with Papa?

HENRIETTA.

I don't know.   (*A thought strikes her.*)   Unless —— (*She goes to the desk and looks through letters that* JANE *placed there.*)   They did!   (*She holds one up.*)   This letter is in Mrs. Jameson's handwriting.

ARABEL.

(*Rising.*)   Whatever shall we do?

HENRIETTA.

(*Dully.*)   There's nothing we *can* do.   We'll have to let them come and be turned out.   I *do* want to see Robert.   Perhaps we can visit with them for a while.

ARABEL.

We can if Papa doesn't get home first.   It's nearly time for him.

HENRIETTA.

Well, if he should come, I hope he won't frighten the child.   But knowing Papa, I'm afraid he will.   (*A door closes off stage* L.   *Both rise quickly.*)   Oh!   Don't tell me that's he!

ARABEL.

I hope not yet.

(*They stand in an attitude of tense waiting, but it is* JANE *who enters with one letter on the tray.*   ARABEL *and* HENRIETTA *relax.*)

HENRIETTA.

Yes, Jane?   (*She sees the letter.*)   What have you there?

JANE.

A letter for Miss Arabel, Miss.

ARABEL.

(*Crossing* L.)   Did it come through the post?   (*She takes the letter.*)

JANE.

(*Roguishly.*)   Oh, no, Miss.   I just stepped out for a moment to go to the green-grocers, and when I was crossing the park a young gentleman stopped me and gave it to me with *particular* instructions to give it to you.

ARABEL.

(*A little confused.*)   All right, Jane.   Thank you.

JANE.

(*Craning toward* ARABEL.)   I think—I *think*, Miss, it's from Mr. ——

ARABEL.

(*Hurriedly.*)   Yes, yes, Jane—never mind!   (*She glances at the letter.*)   It *is* from him, Jane.

JANE.

I thought so, Miss.

HENRIETTA.

What's all this?   (*Suddenly.*)   Arabel!   A *man!*

ARABEL.

Never mind.

HENRIETTA.

You tell me, Jane.

JANE.

I don't think I'd best, Miss Henrietta.

HENRIETTA.

Is he very handsome?

JANE.

Why, how you talk, Miss!   Of course he is.

ARABEL.

(*Quickly.*) *Jane!*

JANE.

(*Ashamed that she fell into the trap.*) Oh! Sorry,
Miss. . . .

HENRIETTA.

So it *is* a man?

ARABEL.

(*Coyly.*) Well, if you must know it's Mr. Richard
Barbour whom I met at Aunt Hedley's a month ago.

HENRIETTA.

I'll wager you're in love with him.

(EDWARD MOULTON-BARRETT *appears unnoticed in the
doorway* L. C. *He stands silent, watching.*)

ARABEL.

(*A little shy.*) Well . . .

HENRIETTA.

(*Sincerely.*) I'm awfully glad for you, Arabel. (*Seri-
ously.*) But you'd better warn him against writing to
you. If Papa should find one of the letters . . . (*She
glances toward the door and sees* BARRETT. *The words
die on her lips and she stands frozen.* ARABEL *and* JANE
sense that something is wrong and look toward the door.
BARRETT *takes a few steps down* L. C., *his eyes on* ARABEL.
She tries to hide the letter, and HENRIETTA, *hoping to
give her time to do so, crosses* L. *to* C. *As she does so,*
ARABEL *crosses* R. *to sofa crumpling letter in her hand.*
*She gives the impression that she is going to hide it in
back of the pillows.*) Good—good evening, Papa. . . .

(BARRETT *ignores her and crossing her, takes the center
of the stage. She moves* L. *and stands before the
chair.* ARABEL *is standing* R. *in front of the sofa, her
back to* BARRETT. JANE, *who has been standing* U. C.
left of the piano, slips from the room.)

BARRETT.

(*In a cold, measured voice, speaking only to* ARABEL.) What have you there? (*Pause.*) What are you trying to conceal?

ARABEL.

(*Half turning.*) Nothing, Papa . . . only . . . a letter. . . .

BARRETT.

(*Extending his hand.*) Give it to me. (*She makes no move. Sharply.*) Did you hear?

HENRIETTA.

(*Placatingly.*) Really, it's nothing, Papa. Arabel only ——

BARRETT.

(*Turning to her. Bitingly.*) I am not speaking to you, Henrietta. I have no business with you. I am addressing your sister. (*Turning back to* ARABEL.) *Give me that note!*

(ARABEL *stands rebelliously hesitating for a brief moment. Gradually she withers before her father's steady scrutiny. She moves* L. *slowly and passes him the letter.*)

ARABEL.

(*Weakly.*) Yes . . . Papa. . . .

(BARRETT *opens the letter and reads it, while* ARABEL *and* HENRIETTA *stand in breathless silence waiting. When he has finished, he looks up at* ARABEL, *who shrinks. There is a brief pause.*)

BARRETT.

(*Quietly.*) So. You have been carrying on this contemptible friendship behind my back. Why? (*With a sudden burst of anger.*) I can tell you why. Because you knew that if I found out about it, I should immediately put a stop to it—that I should forbid you to see or communicate with this man again. And that is to be my exact procedure.

ARABEL.

(*Pleadingly.*) But Papa, I hardly know him. It's a friendship—a very ordinary one—believe me, it is! There's nothing ——

BARRETT.

This letter would seem to indicate a slightly deeper interest on the part of the writer.

ARABEL.

Am I responsible for that? How could I know? . . . Why can't you understand? . . .

BARRETT.

(*Coldly.*) I think I do understand. Young lady, you may go to your room. When you have made up your mind to give me your oath that you will never, in any way, see or communicate with this man again, then you may leave that room. Until that time, I am quite able to dispense with your company.

ARABEL.

Please, Papa, don't think me insolent when I ask you this, but aren't we ever going to be old enough to run our own lives and choose our own friends?

BARRETT.

You may go to your room.

ARABEL.

(*Pleadingly.*) Please, Papa, answer me.

BARRETT.

(*Coldly.*) You may go to your room. (*A pause as* ARABEL *hesitates.*) Well, are you going?

ARABEL.

Yes, Papa. . . . (*She goes toward the door, bursting into tears as she nears it, then exits.*)

HENRIETTA.

May I go with her, Papa?

BARRETT.

(*Decisively.*) No, you may not. What she needs now is solitude in which to think. You will not go near her for the rest of the evening, do you understand?

HENRIETTA.

Yes, Papa, but ——

BARRETT.

See that you obey me. (*He crosses to his desk and seats himself, picking up his letters.* HENRIETTA *comes to him.*)

HENRIETTA.

But, Papa, I should be with her . . . she needs me! She might do something—anything! She might run away ——

BARRETT.

(*Contemptuously.*) Paugh! She hasn't the nerve. It takes more courage than any child of mine has to do a thing like that. Not one of you has any backbone—not one! (*In a quieter voice.*) Yes . . . yes, there *was* one. . . . (*He looks at the picture of Elizabeth on his desk.*) Elizabeth . . . Elizabeth had courage. . . . (*His voice becomes hard again.*) But she sacrificed all right to be called my child. That I think I shall never forget. (*He turns abruptly to the opened letter in his hand and glances at it. His manner indicates that he is trying to forget any sign of weakening he may have shown. Suddenly he sits bolt upright, frowning.*) What's *this?*

HENRIETTA.

What, Papa?

BARRETT.

(*With suppressed anger.*) This letter. It's from Mrs. Jameson. She and her husband are in England—and they've brought Elizabeth's child with them!

HENRIETTA.

(*Faintly.*) Yes . . . Papa?

BARRETT.

(*With rising anger.*) They intend to bring him here— here to this house! Here to see *me!* Confound them for fools—sentimental fools!

HENRIETTA.

Yes, I know. I got a letter from her myself. They're due here any minute. (*Pleadingly.*) Surely you're going to see them, Papa?

BARRETT.

(*Rising abruptly.*) Surely I'm not! When Elizabeth Barrett left this house to marry Robert Browning, she knew that neither she nor any of her family would ever be admitted to it again. I will *not* see the child! That is quite definite!

HENRIETTA.

But, Papa, Ba's not responsible for their coming. Don't blame her and don't blame Robert Browning either.

BARRETT.

I am not blaming anyone, least of all Elizabeth. . . . But I *will not see her son.* (*Peremptorily.*) Get in touch with the Jamesons and tell them not to come.

HENRIETTA.

I can't do that. I don't know where to reach them and they're probably on their way already. (*Going to him. Earnestly.*) Papa, you *must* see them—if only for the child.

BARRETT.

(*Firmly.*) Henrietta, I cannot. I swore I would never see either Ba or her family after she left this house, and I will not break that oath.

HENRIETTA.

Papa, you've *got* to do it. Don't you see? If you refuse to see the child, he will always remember that; it will remain imprinted upon his memory for the rest of his life. And he will hate you . . . because you hate him.

Elizabeth loved you very dearly. . . . How can you allow her son to grow up hating you?

(HENRIETTA'S *words affect* BARRETT *deeply, yet he endeavors not to show it. From his attitude one can see that a struggle is going on within him. Then he reaches a decision; after that one sees the first hint of weakness in this hard man. He suddenly becomes old. His voice, when he speaks, has an unaccustomed tone of weariness.*)

BARRETT.

Very well. . . . Very well. . . . I will see the child. . . . (*He goes to the door slowly; then turns back.*)   Tell me . . . when he comes. . . .   [*He exits.*

(HENRIETTA *goes* L. *to* BARRETT'S *desk and picks up the picture of Elizabeth. Looking down upon it.*)

HENRIETTA.

(*Softly.*)   Dear Ba . . . I've done my best. . . .

(JANE *enters* L. C. *and moves* D. C. *from doorway.*)

JANE.

Miss Henrietta . . .

HENRIETTA.

(*Putting the picture down.*)   Yes, Jane?

JANE.

Please, Miss Henrietta, the people have arrived bringing the little boy.

HENRIETTA.

Very good, Jane.   Go down and bring Master Robert up—alone.

JANE.

He's on the stair-landing, Miss, trying to find out what makes the clock tick. I'll fetch him. (*She goes out.* HENRIETTA *moves* R. *a few steps and stands in front of the piano.* JANE'S *voice can be heard speaking off.*) Master Robert . . . (*There is a pause and then* JANE *enters, propelling the little boy before her.)*   Master Robert Browning, Miss.   [*She exits.*

HENRIETTA.

(*Extending her hand.*)   Hello, Robert. How are you?

ROBERT.

(*Coming down to her and shaking hands.*)   Hello, Aunt . . . Aunt Henrietta? I'm very well, thank you.

HENRIETTA.

(*As they move down* C.)   Splendid. (*Crosses* R. *to sofa leading* ROBERT, *and both sit.*)   Sit down—here beside me. I want to talk to you.

ROBERT.

(*Obediently.*)   Yes, Aunt?

HENRIETTA.

Tell me, how is your father?

ROBERT.

Oh, he's very well . . . only I don't see him much to know—he's busy.

HENRIETTA.

Writing?

ROBERT.

Yes. He writes all the time. Poems, you know. Very *beautiful* poems.

HENRIETTA.

Yes, I know.

ROBERT.

Mrs. Jameson said I was coming to see Grandfather today. Where is he? (*He looks around the room.*)

HENRIETTA.

I'll have Jane tell him you're here. (*She rings the little silver bell on table at* R. *of sofa.*)   Tell me, Robert, have you ever heard anything . . . Has anything ever been said to you about . . .

ROBERT.

(*Quickly.*)   About Grandfather?

HENRIETTA.

Yes.   Yes, about your grandfather.

ROBERT.

Oh, yes, lots.   Mama used to tell me about him.

(JANE *enters.*)

JANE.

You rang, Miss Henrietta?

HENRIETTA.

Will you ask Papa to come here, Jane?

JANE.

(*Astonished.*)   Bring the master . . . here?

HENRIETTA.

Yes, Jane.   Right away.

JANE.

(*Doubtfully.*)   Very well, Miss.   [*She exits.*

HENRIETTA.

What did your mama say about your grandfather, Robert?

ROBERT.

She said he was such a nice man, and that she loved him.   And she said that I'd love him too, if I ever saw him.   (*Frowning.*)   But you know, Aunt Henrietta, it was rather funny . . . I mean, somehow she spoke as if maybe I never *would* see him.   Why did she do that?

HENRIETTA.

(*Hesitatingly.*)   Well, Robert, your grandfather is rather an—*odd* man.   That's what I wanted to speak to you about before you saw him.

ROBERT.

(*Questioningly.*)   Why is he odd?

HENRIETTA.

I don't know, dear. I've often wondered. . . . But because he *is* this way . . . he may not like you exactly at first.

ROBERT.

(*Anxiously.*) Why won't he like me?

HENRIETTA.

(*At a loss.*) I don't know, dear.

ROBERT.

(*Eagerly.*) But I *want* him to like me. I like him. I never saw him, but I saw his picture—Mama had one—and I knew right away I should like him.

HENRIETTA.

I hope you do, Robert. (*Smiling.*) No, I don't *hope* you do—I know you *will*.

(JANE *enters.*)

JANE.

The master says he is coming immediately, Miss.

HENRIETTA.

Thank you, Jane.

JANE.

Yes, Miss.   [*She exits.*

HENRIETTA.

(*Rising.*) I'm going down now and see Mr. and Mrs. Jameson. You can visit with your grandfather alone. And remember . . . (*putting her hand firmly on his shoulder*) don't be afraid of him. Show him you're not frightened of anything he says.

ROBERT.

I won't be scared, Aunt Henrietta. . . . (*Not quite as stoutly.*) I'll . . . try not to be. . . .

HENRIETTA.

Good boy. (*She gives him a reassuring little pat, then goes up to the door and exits.*)

(ROBERT *shuffles a moment and then goes over to the little table at the right of the sofa. He finds there the volume of his mother's poetry, and he is flicking through the pages when* BARRETT *enters. The latter advances down* C., *observing the boy coldly.* ROBERT *looks up from the book and sees his grandfather. He comes slowly* C., *his hand timidly outstretched.*)

ROBERT.

(*Hesitating.*) How . . . how do you do . . . Grandfather?

BARRETT.

(*Bluntly.*) How do you do? (*He looks for a moment over the boy's head. Then he drops his eyes and sees the hand that is still outstretched. He gives it a brief, impersonal little handshake and drops it. Then he goes* L. *and seats himself at his desk.*)

ROBERT.

(*After a moment.*) I've . . . I've come a long . . . a long way to see you . . . Grandfather.

BARRETT.

So I am aware. (*Pause.*) Did you have a pleasant trip?

ROBERT.

(*Hesitating.*) It was all right . . . only . . . only I got seasick.

BARRETT.

(*Brusquely.*) Indeed?

ROBERT.

(*Timidly.*) Yes. I was quite ill. . . .

BARRETT.

Indeed?

ROBERT.

I . . . I can remember lying in the berth and wishing the boat would . . . would stop rolling.

BARRETT.

Unpleasant!

ROBERT.

(*Earnestly.*) Oh, it wasn't nice at all. (*Shyly.*) I didn't like it much. . . .

BARRETT.

Indeed?

ROBERT.

No . . . (*weakly*) not at all. . . . (*Half turns* R., *then turning back suddenly.*) Grandfather, aren't you ever coming to see us in Italy?

BARRETT.

I consider it very unlikely.

ROBERT.

Why?

BARRETT.

(*Sharply.*) I said I considered it very unlikely. Let that be sufficient explanation.

ROBERT.

(*A little frightened.*) Yes, Grandfather. . . . (*Looks at papers* BARRETT *has picked up from his desk.*) What . . . what are you reading, Grandfather?

BARRETT.

Nothing you would understand.

ROBERT.

(*Impulsively.*) Why don't you like me, Grandfather?

BARRETT.

(*Looking up.*) Eh? Who said anything about disliking you? (*Suddenly.*) Who's been talking to you about me? Was it your Aunt Henrietta? *Was it?*

ROBERT.

(*Abashed.*) Oh, no . . . no, really. But you . . .
you—well, you don't *seem* to like me very much.

BARRETT.

Stuff!

ROBERT.

(*Weakly.*) Well, you . . . you don't *act* so. . . .

BARRETT.

(*Irritatedly.*) Indeed? And how would you have me
act?

ROBERT.

(*Hesitating.*) Well . . .

BARRETT.

(*Rising. Emphatically.*) Let me tell you something,
Master Robert Barrett Browning. If I show a dislike for
you, it is because I have good reason to dislike anyone
connected with you or your name. Perhaps you don't
know—perhaps you do—but when your mother was
young she committed an act that was gravely against my
wishes. (*Quietly.*) I loved your mother . . . but I
could not forgive her. (*Decidedly.*) And I find it very
hard to forgive her son.

ROBERT.

(*Stoutly.*) Mother never did anything that was wrong!

BARRETT.

(*Fiercely.*) You dare contradict your grandfather?

ROBERT.

(*Doggedly.*) Yes.

BARRETT.

(*Falls back into his chair, astonished.*) Why?

ROBERT.

(*Earnestly.*) Because I know it's true. She couldn't
have done anything wrong, Grandfather. She couldn't!

She was the best mother in the world. Indeed she was!
(BARRETT *coughs and moves uneasily in his chair.*)
Please don't say anything against her, Grandfather.
Please don't because then I won't like you. . . . (*Walks
a few steps* R. *Shyly.*) And I . . . I want to like you.

BARRETT.

(*Surprised, he speaks gruffly.*) You do, eh?

ROBERT.

Yes, I do. (*Going* L. *to desk.*) And I want you to
like me.

BARRETT.

Well . . . well, I will confess you're a little different
from what I expected. Got a—got a mind of your own.
. . . I admire you for that.

ROBERT.

(*Hopefully.*) Will you like me, Grandfather? Will
you?

BARRETT.

Stuff! Ahem! (*Pause.*) Tell me—tell me, how do
you like England?

ROBERT.

Oh, I like it, Grandfather. (*Dully.*) Only . . . only
sometimes I get lonesome for Father. I was before you
came. Now I'm not so much. (*Confidentially.*) Father
likes England, too. He often wanted to come, but it made
Mama ill to leave Italy so he didn't. So instead of coming, he wrote a poem about being here. I liked the poem.
I learned it by heart.

BARRETT.

Indeed?

ROBERT.

Yes. Do you know the one I mean?

BARRETT.

Of course not. I never read any of your father's
poetry—or your mother's.

ROBERT.

(*Hopefully.*)   May I recite it to you?

BARRETT.

(*Indifferently.*)   You may do as you like.

ROBERT.

(*Resolutely.*)   I will then.   (*Takes center of stage. Clears throat; begins confidently:*)

> " Oh, to be in England
> Now that April's there,
> And whoever wakes in England
> Sees, some morning, unaware
> That the . . .
>   (*Hesitates.*)
> That the . . . that the . . ."

(*Miserably.*)   I've forgotten it, Grandfather.

BARRETT.

Why?   Nothing very difficult about it.   Perfectly simple.   (*Recites thoughtfully:*)

> ". . . Sees some morning, unaware,
> That the lowest boughs and the brushwood sheaf
> Round the elm tree bole are in tiny leaf,
> While the chaffinch sings on the orchard bough
> In England—now ! "

ROBERT.

(*Delightedly.*)   I thought you said you'd never read any of Father's poems, Grandfather !

BARRETT.

(*Confused.*)   Well, I may—I may have glanced through them occasionally.

ROBERT.

(*Vaguely satisfied.*)   Oh.

BARRETT.

Umph !

ROBERT.

I'm going to school, Grandfather.   I'm going to Henley.

BARRETT.

Yes.   Yes, so Mrs. Jameson wrote.

ROBERT.

I don't like it very well, Grandfather. . . . (*Pathetically.*)   I'm . . . I'm kind of scared.   I've . . . I've never been away from home for very long at a time.

(BARRETT *looks at the boy a moment, then leans forward and places his hand on* ROBERT's *shoulder.   The barrier between the two has, for the moment, been let down, and he speaks earnestly.*)

BARRETT.

Robert Browning, let me tell you something.   Don't you be frightened.   Never be that.   No matter what happens, don't turn coward.   If you're courageous, you'll never be beaten.   I shouldn't have to tell you that.   You should have inherited courage from your mother.   She had courage—fine courage—more courage than any of us.   I can see that of your mother in you.   Don't you ever lose it.

ROBERT.

(*Valiantly.*)   I won't, Grandfather.   I'll try not to be afraid—of *anything*.   (BARRETT *gives out another little grunt of approval and again becomes absorbed in his papers, as if he had never spoken.* ROBERT, *after hesitating a moment, picks up the picture on* BARRETT's *desk and looks at it.*)   This . . . this is Mother's picture, isn't it?

BARRETT.

Yes.   Yes, it is.

ROBERT.

It's a good picture of her.

BARRETT.

Indeed?   (*He goes back to his papers.*)

ROBERT.

She had a picture of you on her desk.

BARRETT.

(*Looking up.*)   She . . . she did, eh?

ROBERT.

Oh, yes.   It was always there.

BARRETT.

(*Softly.*)   Really?

ROBERT.

She used to look at it sometimes, and kind of sigh.   I wish she could have seen you before . . . before she went away. . . .   (*He turns from the desk and wipes his eyes on his sleeve.*)

BARRETT.

(*Uncomfortably.*)   Yes.   Yes.   Well—never mind. . . .

(ROBERT *walks* R., *and* BARRETT *looks after him a moment worriedly.   Then* ROBERT, *quite back to normal, spies a large volume in the bookcase.*)

ROBERT.

What's that, Grandfather?

BARRETT.

What's what?

ROBERT.

(*Pointing.*)   That book.

BARRETT.

Oh, that.   That's full of family paintings—little water-color copies of the original oil portraits.

ROBERT.

May I look at it?

BARRETT.

If you wish.

(ROBERT *goes to the bookcase and drags out the big volume.   He takes it to the sofa and sits, holding it in his lap.   Then he opens it and begins turning the pages slowly.   Suddenly he breaks into a giggle.*)

ROBERT.

Who's this funny looking man with the curls, Grandfather?

BARRETT.

Who? (*He rises and crosses* R. *and seats himself beside* ROBERT.) Oh, him. That's a picture of my great-great-grandfather. He was the first of the family to settle in Jamaica. He . . . he was a slave trader. There's rather a long story connected with him.

ROBERT.

What is it, Grandfather?

(JANE *enters and comes a little down* C.)

BARRETT.

Well, I'm not sure how true it is. . . . (*He glances up and sees* JANE *smiling at them. He moves as far from* ROBERT *as he can and scowls fiercely. To* JANE.) Yes, yes. What do you want?

JANE.

Please, sir, Mrs. Jameson says they'll have to take Master Robert now.

BARRETT.

Very well. He'll be down in a moment.

JANE.

Yes, sir.   [*She exits.*

ROBERT.

(*Ruefully.*) I suppose you won't be able to tell me the story of your great-great-grandfather now, will you, Grandfather?

BARRETT.

No, I suppose not.

ROBERT.

(*After a pause.*) Well . . . I've got to go now.

(BARRETT *rises, takes the book from* ROBERT, *puts it on the piano, and walks to* C.)

BARRETT.

Yes. Yes, of course.

ROBERT.

(*Rising.*) Can I come again, Grandfather?

BARRETT.

I see no reason why you shouldn't.

ROBERT.

Thank you, Grandfather. And will you tell me more about those funny men in the book?

BARRETT.

I'll see.

ROBERT.

Thank you, Grandfather.

BARRETT.

(*With a trace of impatience.*) Stop thanking me!

ROBERT.

Yes, Grandfather. (*Going a few steps* L. *with hand outstretched.*) Good-bye, Grandfather.

BARRETT.

(*A little regretfully.*) Good-bye. (*He shakes hands.*)

ROBERT.

(*Eagerly.*) Will you tell me about your great-great-grandfather when I come again?

BARRETT.

Yes. Yes, I will. (*Suddenly.*) Oh, here—(*he takes a coin from his pocket and passes it to* ROBERT) here's half a crown for you. (*Quickly.*) And don't thank me! Just don't lose it!

ROBERT.

(*Happily.*) I *knew* I'd like you, Grandfather!

BARRETT.

(*Uncomfortably.*) Yes—yes, well—ahem!

(ROBERT *crosses and goes up* L. *to door. There he turns and smiles shyly.* BARRETT *watches him.*)

ROBERT.

Good-bye, Grandfather.

BARRETT.

Good-bye. (*With another little smile,* ROBERT *exits.* BARRETT *waits a moment and then slowly goes up* L. *to the door. He leans rather wearily, with one hand against the door casing, looking out. Then he turns and slowly comes down to his desk. He sees Elizabeth's picture and stares at it for a moment. Then, giving his shoulders an impatient shrug, he mutters " Stuff " under his breath, seats himself, and turns his attention to his papers.* HENRIETTA *enters on tiptoe and crosses* R. *to sofa. She picks up her scarf which has been hanging over the back, and turns to retrace her steps.* BARRETT *suddenly becomes conscious of her presence and looks up. He speaks quietly.*) Henrietta.

HENRIETTA.

(*Starting back and catching her breath.*) Yes, Papa. . . .

BARRETT.

Where are you going?

HENRIETTA.

Nowhere, Papa. . . .

BARRETT.

(*Sharply.*) Don't lie to me, Henrietta! Where are you going?

(HENRIETTA *hesitates.* ARABEL *enters and goes to her sister's side. At sight of her* BARRETT *rises.*)

ARABEL.

Don't blame her, Papa.

HENRIETTA.

Arabel, be quiet!

ARABEL.

She—she was going out with me!

BARRETT.

(*Coldly.*) I was under the impression, young lady, that I had confined you to your room.

ARABEL.

You did, Papa, but ——

HENRIETTA.

(*Quickly.*) But I persuaded her to go out in spite of you.

BARRETT.

(*With suppressed anger.*) Indeed? And for what reason should you, Henrietta, take it upon yourself to openly incite your sister to further disobedience?

HENRIETTA.

Because you're neither reasonable nor fair!

BARRETT.

Let me be the judge of that!

HENRIETTA.

(*Vehemently.*) All you think of is your duty! You think it your duty to punish us—to make us cringe in fear!

BARRETT.

(*Sharply.*) *Henrietta!* (*Quietly.*) Where were you going?

HENRIETTA.

(*Slowly and intensely.*) We intend to meet the man who wrote Arabel the letter you saw and read. He asked her for an appointment. We were going to keep it.

BARRETT.

(*Softly.*) So . . . it has come to open rebellion. . . . My own daughters defy me. (*Abruptly turning to* ARA-BEL.) Arabel, you may go back to your room. I will deal with you later. (*He pauses, then looks at* HENRIETTA *meaningly.*) Just at present, I wish a private interview with your sister.

ARABEL.

(*With a sudden rush of feeling.*) I won't go back, Papa! I *won't!* I *want* to meet this man you unjustly hate! Why shouldn't I meet him? I like him—I love him! Now you know. I love him! I said I didn't, but I do! I intend to see him now and every chance I get! It's only natural—it's only human!

BARRETT.

(*Furiously.*) SILENCE!

ARABEL.

(*Defiantly.*) I won't be silent! I *won't!* (*Suddenly pleading.*) Can't you understand, Papa? Don't you know the meaning of the word "love"? Isn't there anything which you care for, if only the least little bit? Is there nothing for which you have some affection? Enough so that you can understand what I feel . . . what I hope? Tell me, Papa, isn't there?

(BARRETT *stands silently looking at the floor for a moment. Then he sighs, and raises his eyes to Elizabeth's picture. He looks long at this, and as he looks he seems to see something which no one else can see. Softly, he speaks.*)

BARRETT.

" . . . Sees some morning, unaware,
That the lowest boughs and the brushwood sheaf
Round the elm tree bole are in tiny leaf,
While the chaffinch sings . . ."

(*With a little frown.*) Nothing very difficult about that. . . . Perfectly simple. . . .

ARABEL.

(*Puzzled.*) I—I beg pardon . . . Papa?

(BARRETT *starts, as if awakening from a dream. He*

looks at ARABEL *for a second, then recalls what is happening, and straightens himself.*)

BARRETT.

Oh, yes. Yes, Arabel. (*He pauses a moment, then suddenly seems to reach a decision.*) Arabel, if you wish you may bring this man Barbour here to the house. . . . (*Quickly.*) I cannot say that my conscience approves the act, but . . . (*slowly*) but if you want to . . . you may bring him. . . .

ARABEL.

(*Astonished.*) You mean——

BARRETT.

(*Impatiently.*) You heard what I said! (*To* HENRI-ETTA.) Henrietta, you had best accompany your sister. She should be chaperoned.

ARABEL.

(*Almost in tears from joy.*) Papa—oh, Papa!

BARRETT.

(*Sharply.*) Silence! If you're going you'd best go, before I alter my decision. I *despise* myself for my weakness! (*With an impatient gesture of dismissal.*) Get out!

HENRIETTA and ARABEL.

Yes, Papa!   [*They exit joyfully.*

(BARRETT *looks after them for a moment. Then he crosses* R. *wearily, to stand in front of the sofa. Now he seems older than he has ever seemed and more lonely. After a moment, he sees the book of Eliza-beth's poetry on the table, and picks it up. Looking at it thoughtfully, he speaks quietly.*)

BARRETT.

Poems . . . by Elizabeth Barrett Browning. . . . (*He runs through the pages slowly. Then he very wearily lowers himself onto the sofa, and settles back to read. After a pause he begins to speak aloud. Reading:*)

* " How do I love thee? Let me count the ways.
 I love thee to the depth and breadth and height
 My soul can reach, when feeling out of sight
 For the ends of Being and Ideal Grace.
 I love thee to the level of everyday's
 Most quiet need, by sun and candle light.
 I love thee freely, as men strive for Right;
 I love thee purely, as they turn from Praise.
 I love thee with the passion put to use
 In my old grief and in my childhood's faith.
 I love thee with a love I seem to lose
 With my lost saints—I love thee with the breath,
 Smiles, tears, of all my life!—and if God choose,
 I shall but love thee better after death."

(BARRETT *slowly looks up from the book and pauses a moment. He sees the picture of Elizabeth on his desk. He closes the book, puts it aside, and slowly rises. He crosses* L. *with slow step to the desk, and picks up the picture. After a moment he repeats softly:*)

" I shall but love thee better . . . after death. . . ."

SLOW CURTAIN

* It may be felt that the recital of the entire poem above may drag a little. If so, the actor may recite merely the last four lines.

PROPERTY PLOT

HENRIETTA. Basket of embroidery, watch pinned to her dress, silver bell (on end table), scarf (on sofa).

ARABEL. Book of Elizabeth Barrett Browning's poems, scarf.

JANE. Silver tray and letters.

BARRETT. Half-crown piece.

ROBERT. Picture album (in bookcase).

SETTING

The drawing room at 50 Wimpole Street, London, is a lofty, high-ceilinged room, darkly panelled in oak in excellent taste. The furniture, of mid-Victorian period, is heavy and uncomfortable. There are long windows, heavily draped, at R. A dark, heavy gold-framed family portrait in oils hangs on the wall in the center above the panelling. There is a sofa down R., with a small table beside it, while against the wall rear is a bookcase. Down L. is a writing table with a chair behind it and one beside it, R. Up C. there may be, if desired, a piano. The only entrance to the room is through the door up L.

MUSICAL EFFECTS

It has been found impressive, but not essential, to ring up our curtain to the first six or eight measures of Tschaikowsky's "None But a Lonely Heart." This musical score is also effective in closing the performance, as background for the last lines of the poem, "How Do I Love Thee?"

No one shall make any changes in this title(s) for the purpose of production. No part of this book may be reproduced, stored in a retrieval system, scanned, uploaded, or transmitted in any form, by any means, now known or yet to be invented, including mechanical, electronic, digital, photocopying, recording, videotaping, or otherwise, without the prior written permission of the publisher. No one shall share this title(s), or any part of this title(s), through any social media or file hosting websites.

For all inquiries regarding motion picture, television, online/digital and other media rights, please contact Concord Theatricals Corp.

MUSIC AND THIRD-PARTY MATERIALS USE NOTE

Licensees are solely responsible for obtaining formal written permission from copyright owners to use copyrighted music and/or other copyrighted third-party materials (e.g., artworks, logos) in the performance of this play and are strongly cautioned to do so. If no such permission is obtained by the licensee, then the licensee must use only original music and materials that the licensee owns and controls. Licensees are solely responsible and liable for clearances of all third-party copyrighted materials, including without limitation music, and shall indemnify the copyright owners of the play(s) and their licensing agent, Concord Theatricals Corp., against any costs, expenses, losses and liabilities arising from the use of such copyrighted third-party materials by licensees. For music, please contact the appropriate music licensing authority in your territory for the rights to any incidental music.

IMPORTANT BILLING AND CREDIT REQUIREMENTS

If you have obtained performance rights to this title, please refer to your licensing agreement for important billing and credit requirements.